CatDog Tales #1

A SPACE ODDITY

by Steven Banks

Simon Spotlight/Nickelodeon

New York   London   Toronto   Sydney   Singapore

Based on the TV series *CatDog*®
created by Peter Hannan as seen on Nickelodeon®

SIMON SPOTLIGHT
An imprint of Simon & Schuster Children's Publishing Division
1230 Avenue of the Americas, New York, New York 10020

Copyright © 2000 Viacom International Inc.
All rights reserved. NICKELODEON, *CatDog,* and all related titles, logos, and
characters are trademarks of Viacom International Inc.

All rights reserved including the right of reproduction in whole or in part in any form.

SIMON SPOTLIGHT and colophon are registered trademarks of Simon & Schuster.

Manufactured in the United States of America

First Edition
2 4 6 8 10 9 7 5 3 1

ISBN 0-689-83363-6

Library of Congress Catalog Card Number 00-30190

chapter 1

CatDog was going to Mars.

Now going to Mars was the last thing that CatDog thought would happen to them when they woke up that morning.

The day started like any other CatDog day. They woke up in their bed. Cat was grouchy. Dog was happy. Dog had a big bowl of Mean Bob cereal, pancakes, moldy meat, and a bone for breakfast. Cat had hot tea and tuna on toast. Dog ate quickly, which was usual for him. But today Cat ate quickly too. CatDog had to be at city hall at 10 A.M. sharp.

CatDog and everyone else in Nearburg had been summoned to city hall to hear Mayor Rancid Rabbit make an important announcement. The Greasers—Cliff, Shriek, and Lube—were there, along with Mervis, Dunglap, and Mr. Sunshine.

On the steps of city hall was a podium with a microphone, flags, banners, and an enormous blue curtain.

"What do you think the big announcement is gonna be, Cat?" asked Dog.

"Probably something boring," Cat said, yawning, thinking this might be a good time for a catnap.

"Maybe he's gonna announce it's Free Bones for Dogs Day!" Dog said, his mouth watering at the thought of bones.

"Dog, you just ate!" complained Cat.

"That was ten minutes ago!" Dog protested.

A limousine roared up, and out stepped

Mayor Rancid, followed by Lola Caricola, CatDog's friend and Nearburg's head scientist.

"*Hola,* Lola!" shouted Dog from the crowd. Lola waved to CatDog.

Rancid stepped up to the microphone and tapped it with his paw. "Testing . . . testing . . . testing! Hey, is this thing on?"

The microphone shrieked, making a really loud, high, squeaky noise. Everyone put their hands over their ears.

"Why does that always happen?" growled Cat.

Rancid cleared his throat and spoke. "Today is the greatest day in Nearburg history!"

Wait a minute, Cat thought, it's not my birthday.

Rancid continued. "I present to you the greatest thing you have ever laid your eyes upon! Behold . . . the Really Rancid Rocket Ship!"

The curtain parted to reveal a giant, super-shiny, supersonic rocket ship.

"Ooooooohhhhhhhh!" went the crowd.

The rocket was taller than the tallest building in Nearburg. Painted on its side was an enormous picture of Rancid himself, with a broad and sparkly rabbit-tooth smile.

"The Really Rancid Rocket Ship was built and designed by the brilliant scientist, our own Lola Caricola!" said Rancid.

Lola waved her wing at the crowd as they clapped and cheered.

"And paid for by your generous tax dollars!" said Rancid. "We will be sending two brave astronauts on a thirty-five million-mile journey to Mars."

Lola flew up to the microphone. "Where we will conduct many scientific experiments and conduct research and—"

Rancid grabbed the microphone. "The future is now, ladies and gentlemen! We're going to Mars!"

"Hi-ho-diggety!" shouted Dog. "We're going to Mars, Cat! Let's start packing!"

Cat sighed. "Dog, we're not going to Mars. Two astronauts are going to Mars."

"But I wanna go to Mars. I wanna be an astronaut!" said Dog.

Rancid motioned to CatDog to quiet down. "Be quiet! I have a very important golf game to play in five minutes, so listen up. I'm going to need two brave, strong, and intelligent astronauts for this mission. They will have the great honor of being the first people to land on Mars and plant the Nearburg flag! I'm looking for the toughest, strongest, best, and brightest! All applicants should report to Rancid's Aeronautical Space Association tomorrow morning at 7 A.M. sharp!"

On their way home, Cat laughed. "What kind of nut would want to sit in a giant rocket and blast off into space?"

"Me! Me! Me!" shouted Dog.

Cat sighed. "I forgot about you."

Lola was excited, talking to Rancid in the limousine as they drove away. "Rancid, you did a great thing for science!"

"Yeah, yeah, yeah . . . it's always been my lifelong goal to make the world a better place," said Rancid, smiling to himself. He didn't care if Lola thought this was a scientific mission. Rancid had other plans. Big plans.

chapter 2

That night at home, Dog was so excited, he was still bouncing around the room.

"Cat! We gotta be astronauts!"

"No, we don't!" replied Cat.

"But it's the chance to boldly go where no CatDog has ever gone before!"

"Forget it!" said Cat. "This CatDog isn't going anywhere! Space travel is too dangerous. Think of what could happen up there! We could get stranded on a strange planet! Lost in space! Go into a black hole and never come out!"

"But we could have a neat adventure like my all-time favorite super-action hero Mean Bob did in my all-time favorite movie, *Mean Bob in Space, Part 12!*"

"No, no, no! And that's final!" said Cat.

Just then Winslow popped out of his hole. "I agree with Cat! He's one hundred percent correct!"

Cat and Dog both looked at Winslow in shock. Winslow never agreed with Cat.

"See?" said Cat. "Even Winslow agrees with me!"

Winslow hopped up onto the kitchen table. "Cat is way too delicate to survive in space. He ain't got the right stuff!"

Cat puffed out his chest. "Now wait a minute, rat boy, I got the right stuff! I could be an astronaut!"

Winslow smiled. "So why ain't you goin'?"

Cat stammered, "Well . . . because . . . "

Cat looked over at the calendar on their

kitchen wall. "Because I'm getting my yarn ball collection cleaned that day," he said. "They need their annual hot waxing."

Winslow scratched his tiny blue chin. "Well, it's probably better you don't go, Cat. Think about it. If you went to Mars you'd have to put up with all that fame and fortune."

Cat's eyes instantly lit up like a Christmas tree. "Fame and fortune?"

Winslow continued. "If you go to Mars, everyone will wanna meet you, get your autograph, you'll be on TV, and they'll probably have a big parade!"

"P-pa-parade . . . ?" stammered Cat as he imagined himself in a limousine going down Main Street with everyone waving at him.

"Sure!" said Winslow. "And don't forget product endorsements, TV commercials, getting your face on collectible plates, dolls, coins, toys! And then you'd have all that money and you'd have to figure out what to do with it! You're right, Cat, you don't want that kinda fame and fortune!"

Cat hadn't thought about all that. This was a different story. The chance for fame and fortune had completely slipped his mind. He reminded himself never to let that happen again. Going into space would be risky, but he couldn't risk losing this chance of a lifetime!

"Dog!" announced Cat. "We're going to Mars!"

"But what about your annual yarn ball waxing?" asked Dog.

Cat struck a heroic pose and proclaimed, "Sometimes in life you have to make sacrifices!"

chapter 3

The next morning CatDog arrived bright and early at the front gate of Rancid's Aeronautical Space Association, RASA for short. It was a big building with another big picture of Rancid painted on the front. Under his picture it said "RASA—A DIVISION OF RANCID RABBIT, INC. MAKING THE WORLD A BETTER PLACE IN SPACE BECAUSE HE CARES."

Cat and Dog weren't the only ones who wanted to be astronauts and go to Mars. When they walked up to the entrance they saw Cliff, Lube, and Shriek leaning against the gate.

"Hey, look! It's CatDog!" bellowed Cliff. "What the heck are you doin' here? You come to meet a real, live astronaut?"

Shriek whispered to Dog, "Hey, brown eyes, you come to wish me luck?"

Lube turned to Cliff. "Duh . . . why are we here, Cliff?"

Cliff sighed. "Lube, you numbskull! I told ya twenty times, we're here to be astronauts!"

Lube smiled. "Yummy. I like nuts."

"We're here to be astronauts too!" proclaimed Dog.

The Greasers looked at each other, and then they all fell down on the ground laughing. The laughed so hard that tears streamed down their faces.

"What's so darn funny?" demanded Cat.

"You is funny!" said Cliff, wiping a tear from his eye. "And you as an astronaut is even funnier! Who'd send a freak like you into space?"

"Laugh all you want. We're going to Mars!" said Cat.

"In your dreams!" said Cliff, poking his finger in Cat's chest. "You're a big scaredy-cat! You'd wet your pants as soon as they started counting ten, nine, eight . . . and whatever comes after that."

"Two," said Lube.

"We're twice as tough as you!" said Dog.

"You won't last two minutes!" barked Cliff.

"We'll see about that!" said Cat. "It's between us and you guys!"

"I'm not a guy!" screeched Shriek.

Just then up walked the very short and very green and very serious Mr. Sunshine. "Is this where we sign up to go to Mars?"

Right behind Mr. Sunshine came CatDog's friends, Mervis and Dunglap, talking excitedly.

"Oh, I hope we get to wear those shiny silver space suits!" squealed Mervis.

"I just wanna be weightless and float around," said Dunglap.

"I can't wait!" said Mervis as he jumped up and down with excitement.

"Careful, Mervis. Don't hurt yourself before we start!" warned Dunglap.

"I'm not gonna hurt myself," said Mervis just as he tripped over a rock and stubbed his toe. "Ow! The pain! The agony!"

Cat looked at Mr. Sunshine, Mervis, and Dunglap. "You all want to go to Mars, too?"

"Why shouldn't we?" argued Dunglap.

"It's been my lifelong dream," said Mr. Sunshine.

"You're all wastin' your time!" growled Cliff. "The only people goin' to Mars are the Greasers!"

"Cliff, you can't all go," said Cat. "There's three of you! They only want two people."

"Lube don't count as a complete person," said Shriek.

"Yeah!" said Lube proudly.

Everyone started yelling and arguing and saying why they would be chosen to go to Mars, when Rancid appeared at the gate.

Rancid blew a loud whistle. "Okay! Okay! Settle down! So you want to be astronauts, eh? Then listen up! We're going to put you through the toughest seven days of your miserable lives! We don't want any crybabies! No momma's boys! No daddy's girls! We're going to run you ragged! We're going to stretch your bodies to the limit!"

Dog proudly raised his paw. "Cat and I can stretch real good! In fact, one time we stretched all the way from Nearburg to Farburg!"

Cliff laughed. "Yeah! Dat's cuz we wuz pulling you from each end!"

"That was amazingly beautiful!" said Shriek.

"That was amazingly painful!" said Cat.

"Mervis and I played jump rope on you!" said Dunglap.

"I hurt myself three times!" said Mervis.

"I took a lovely photograph of them. It's hanging in my bedroom," said Mr. Sunshine.

Rancid glared at them. "Wonderful! Are we all through with our little trip down memory lane?"

Everyone nodded.

"Good!" Rancid continued. "At the end of those seven days, if you're still alive, we will choose two lucky stiffs to make history and go to Mars!"

Cat nudged Dog. "And those two lucky stiffs are going to be us!"

Rancid leaned forward and narrowed his eyes. "But I want to warn you, right here, right now, that this is no picnic in the park! This is a very dangerous and risky mission. No one has ever gone to Mars before!"

Dog raised his hand. "Excuse me, Mr. Rancid, sir! Mean Bob went to Mars in his classic movie *Mean Bob Goes to Mars, Part V: The Special Edition with Scenes That Weren't Very Good but We Added Them So You Would Pay to See the Movie Again Even Though You Own It on Video!*"

"I'm talking about reality, pooch!" said Rancid. "As I was saying, it's a dangerous mission—"

"I ain't afraid of nuthin'!" yelled Cliff.

"What about that little monkey toy that makes the funny noise that you made Lube throw away?" asked Shriek.

"I told you never to bring that up!" whispered Cliff.

"May I continue?" yelled Rancid. "There is always the possibility of failure in a mission like this. You might not come back. You might not survive. That's why *I'm* not going."

Cat was getting a little nervous. This was

sounding a lot scarier than he thought it would be. He whispered to Dog, "Maybe going to Mars isn't such a good idea, Dog."

"You're not getting scared, are you?" asked Dog.

"No, of course not!" said Cat. "But we might miss some really good TV shows while we're away on Mars. I think that new show *Eraser Boy* is going to be on."

"We can tape it!" said Dog. "Shhh!"

"But without risk, there are no rewards!" continued Rancid. "Remember: No guts . . . no glory! No pain . . . no fame!"

Cat thought to himself, Fame. That's right. Keep thinking about fame, Cat. Fame. Glory. Money. And that parade. My wonderful, glorious parade . . .

"So," asked Rancid, "who wants to be an astronaut?"

Everyone raised their hand. Except Lube. He raised his foot.

chapter 4

The next week was the toughest week CatDog had ever endured. On the first day, everyone took turns riding in a very fast machine called the Supersonic Spinner That Might Make You Throw Up. It was designed to test everyone's reaction to space travel.

Each person sat in a little chair that was attached to a long pole. When Lola pushed a button, the chair went around and around the edge of the room, in a circle, very fast.

CatDog rode it first. Together, of course.

Dog loved it. "Hi-ho-diggety! I wanna go again! Faster! Faster! Make it go faster!" he yelled.

"That's as fast as it goes!" called Lola.

Cat didn't like the Supersonic Spinner. He got dizzy, very dizzy. His face went green. His eyes watered, and he wanted to throw up.

But as he was spinning around and around, Cat kept reminding himself of the fame and fortune that awaited him. He closed his eyes tight and pictured himself sitting on top of a float with thousands of people cheering and clapping and chanting, "Cat! Cat! Cat!"

The other astronauts-to-be didn't fare so well either.

Dunglap threw up.

Poor Mervis forgot to put on his seat belt and was thrown out of the chair.

Mr. Sunshine fell asleep when he went around.

The Greasers all rode at the same time, arguing over who could stay on the longest.

To make sure they were all physically fit, Lola tested each person to see how many push-ups they could do. Cliff did 1,078 push-ups. Lola finally had to stop him so everyone else could have a turn.

"Hey! Whattaya doin'?" protested Cliff. "I just got started here! I can do two thousand! With one hand!"

Cat could only do five push-ups, but since Dog did ninety-five, they counted it as a grand total of one hundred for CatDog.

Mervis and Dunglap each did fifty. Mervis kept banging his nose on the floor.

Poor Mr. Sunshine could only do one, so Lola had to send him away.

"Oh, well," he said mournfully, "maybe next year."

However, the very next day Mr. Sunshine joined the Nearburg World Gym. He exercised and exercised, night and day. Six months later he won third place in the Mr. Nearburg Muscle Man Contest . . . but that's another story.

Later in the week, while they were resting after having been thrown up in the air to see how they fell (Cat did very well, landing on his feet every single time), Dog asked Lola a question. "What if we discover Martians on Mars?"

Everybody laughed.

"Dog, what a silly question!" said Cat.

"Quiet!" said Lola. "The only silly question is the one you already know the answer to. Dog, there has never been evidence of any kind of life-form on Mars."

"But what if we discover one?" asked Dog.

"Bring him home and keep him for a pet," said Cliff.

"Sell him to the zoo!" said Shriek.

"Get his autograph!" said Cat.

Everyone laughed, except Dog.

They all practiced operating the spaceship. Inside the ship was a cockpit, a sleeping area, a computer room, and a big, empty storage room for all the rock samples they were to bring back.

When Lola built the spaceship, she had told Rancid that the storage room was too big. "I only need about ten pounds of rock samples," she said. "That's more than enough to study and put on exhibit at the Nearburg Museum of Cool, Neat Stuff. Why do we need so many rocks?"

"I like rocks," Rancid replied.

The rest of the week was an endless series of tests and exercising and classes. Lola poked the hopeful astronaut candidates, prodded them, stretched them, flipped them, and even gave them shots, which no one liked—except Mervis, for some strange reason.

They took many classes: How to Go to the Bathroom in Space; How Not to Go to the Bathroom in Space; Gravity: Your Friend or Foe?; Landing Is Better than Crashing; The Complete History of Mars; and many others.

Everyone was given points for how well they did in each class and each test. The two Nearburg citizens with the highest scores at the end of the week would be the chosen astronauts.

Finally the very long week came to an end.

Rancid stood at the front of the classroom as the Greasers, Mervis, Dunglap, and CatDog sat in their seats, anxiously awaiting the announcement.

"I have all your scores!" said Rancid, holding up a piece of paper. "It's time to announce who will be the two astronauts. The two who will sail into history! The two who will live in the annals of history! The two who will do Nearburg proud! The two who will—"

"Get on with it!" yelled Cliff. He had to go to the bathroom.

Rancid scowled. "All right! The two astronauts will be: Dog and Mervis!"

"WHAT?" yelled Cat.

Dog and Mervis! That was impossible!

Mervis was crying, he was so happy. "I'm the happiest pig in the world!"

Dog turned to Cat. "Sorry, Cat. Would you like me to bring you back a Mars rock?"

Cat ignored Dog and tapped Rancid on the shoulder. "Excuse me, Rancid, I hate to bring this up, but have you forgotten that I am attached to this Dog? We are stuck together forever! We are connected! United! Merged! Combined! Conjoined!"

"Hmmm," said Rancid. "That is a problem. I guess we'll have to have an operation. Lola! Get in here with a scalpel!"

"What?" yelled a terrified Cat.

Lola flew in. "What's going on?" she asked.

Mervis didn't hear any of this. He was so excited that he tried to do a cartwheel. He always tried to do cartwheels when he got excited. Unfortunately he was the worst cartwheeler in Nearburg and Farburg. Mervis went up in the air and came crashing down on his left leg.

Mervis screamed in pain, "OW! MY LEG!"

"I told you never to do cartwheels again!" scolded Dunglap.

Lola rushed up to examine Mervis. "I'm sorry, Mervis. It's broken. You can't go into space like this."

Mervis began to cry. Dunglap patted him on the shoulder.

Cliff elbowed his way to the front. "So, Rancid! Who's going up in space now?"

Rancid looked at his notes, "Well, let's see, the third highest score belongs to . . . Cat."

Dog jumped for joy. "Cat! You get to go, too!"

Cat smiled. He was going to Mars.

"You're sendin' a lousy CatDog to Mars?" shouted Cliff. "What is dis country coming to? I'm outta here!"

"Me too!" shouted Shriek as she followed Cliff toward the door.

"Who wants to go to stupid old Mars, anyway, and be a stupid astronaut!" shouted Cliff.

"Duh . . . when do we get the nuts?" asked Lube.

chapter 5

CatDog was to blast off the next morning at 8 A.M. Nearburg Standard Time. That night, as they lay in bed, they were so excited, they could hardly sleep.

Winslow popped in. "So you two are going to the big red planet in the sky, eh?"

"That's right, rat boy!" said Cat. "And if you're lucky I might even wave to you when they give us our big parade when we return as heroes!"

Winslow ignored Cat and jumped up

next to Dog, "Hey, bowser, mind if I tag along on your trip?"

Cat looked at Winslow, shocked. "To quote yourself, Winslow, 'What're you, nuts?' We can't take you!"

"I'd like to take you, Winslow," said Dog, "but it's astronauts only."

Winslow shrugged his shoulders. "No harm in asking. Well, nighty-night. Sleep tight. And don't have any nightmares about the *millions* of horrible things that could happen to you up there in space! Heh! Heh! Heh!"

Winslow disappeared into his hole.

CatDog was silent.

Finally Dog spoke up. "Cat, could a million horrible things happen up there?" he asked worriedly.

"No!" said Cat, pulling the blanket over his head. "Lola's a brilliant scientist and she's built an excellent spaceship. We are two highly trained astronauts who, when we return, will be *very* famous and *very* rich. So go to sleep!"

"Okay!" Dog said, and he immediately went to sleep and began to snore.

Cat fell asleep and dreamed of his heroic return from Mars.

chapter 6

The next morning was clear, bright, and beautiful. Not a cloud in the sky. A perfect day for a blastoff. CatDog was strapped into their seats inside the spaceship. In front of them were hundreds of buttons and lights and switches and levers and controls. They were wearing their special space suit that Lola had made for them: one big suit with two helmets.

Lola and Rancid were at Mission Control, a special building next to the launch pad. Lola would be there the whole time, sitting at a control panel. Both she and Rancid were wearing headphones with microphones so they could talk to CatDog.

"This is Lola at Mission Control, CatDog. All systems are go. We are ready to commence countdown in five minutes."

Inside the ship, Dog saluted. "Everything okay here!" he called out.

All of Nearburg was watching the big blastoff on TV or listening to it on the radio. A large crowd had assembled on Cocoaburg Beach, where the spaceship would blast off, to watch with telescopes and binoculars.

The whole town was excited and proud.

Except for the Greasers. They were not excited and they were definitely not proud. They were jealous and angry.

Cliff pointed at the TV showing CatDog in the spaceship. "Dose bums! Dat shoulda been us up in that spaceship!"

"We wuz robbed!" shrieked Shriek.

Lube looked up. "Duh . . . what did they steal?" he asked.

"Nothing! It's just an expression, Lube," explained Shriek. "It means we should be goin' to Mars, not that darn CatDog!"

Cliff banged his fist on the arm of the sofa so hard that he broke the sofa. "Dat lousy CatDog! If I wasn't so mad, I'd . . . I'd . . . cry!"

Back at Mission Control, Lola had finished making her last-minute checks. "We are ready to commence countdown, CatDog!"

"Let's light this firecracker and blow!" said Dog.

"That's a 'go,' CatDog!" said Lola. "Commence countdown! One minute and counting!"

"Here we go, Cat!" called out an excited Dog. He turned to give Cat a thumbs-up sign and he couldn't believe what he saw.

Cat was making a phone call!

"Hey, Marty baby, it's Cat! Listen, on the action-figure toy of me in my space suit, make sure the face looks exactly like mine: extrahandsome! And the cookies in the shape of me as an astronaut, call them Cat-O-Naut cookies and here's the slogan: They're out of this world!"

Dog grabbed the phone from Cat. "Get off the phone! We're about to blast off!"

Cat grabbed the phone back. "Keep your space suit on, Dog! I'm taking care of serious business!"

"Blasting off is serious business!"

"But I'm talking to my agent, Dog!"

Lola's voice came over the speaker. "We are commencing countdown now! Ten, nine, eight . . . "

Cat spoke back into the telephone, "Catch you later, Marty. I gotta do this little blastoff thing."

"Seven, six, five . . ." counted Lola.

"Don't forget the TV miniseries of my life," purred Cat into the phone.

"Four, three . . ." counted Lola.

"Cat! Hang up!" yelled Dog.

"Later, Marty," said Cat. "Don't ever change! You're the best! Love ya! Don't forget my parade! Bye!"

"Two, one . . ." said Lola.

"CAT!" screamed Dog, "You're supposed to be paying attention to our job!"

Cat slyly smiled. "I am."

"Ignition! We have liftoff!" announced Lola.

The rocket blasted off.

It was the loudest noise that CatDog had ever heard.

A gigantic cloud of smoke and flames poured out of the bottom of the rocket as it lifted up into the air. Slowly at first; then the rocket sped faster and faster as it got higher and higher, shooting up through the clouds.

CatDog looked down at Nearburg through the window. It was getting smaller and smaller.

"Hey! I can see our house from here!" said Dog. "Good-bye, house! Good-bye, Nearburg! Be back soon!"

Earth got smaller and smaller until it looked like a little blue marble. As Cat looked down at Earth, he thought that everyone on the planet would soon know his name and admire him. They'd want to meet him and be like him. This was going to be *so* sweet!

chapter 7

"Are we there yet?" asked Dog.

"No, Dog. We have thirty-five million miles to go."

Dog got out of his seat belt and began to float around in the capsule. He loved being weightless. "Wow! You gotta try this, Cat!"

"No, thanks," said Cat as he sat and figured out how much money he should charge for the Mars Cat Souvenir Diet Soda with seventeen different collectible pictures of himself on them.

Dog floated around the spaceship doing

flips, twirls, and cartwheels. After a few hours of this, he got hungry. "Food! Food! Food!" he barked.

"Excellent idea, Dog. I'm famished!"

"Break out the space food!" said Dog as he floated a plastic bag filled with brown squishy stuff toward Cat.

Cat made a face as he looked at the bag. "What is that?"

"Hot turkey and stuffing with cranberry sauce and mashed potatoes with gravy and green beans and pumpkin pie with whipped cream!" Dog said, his mouth watering at the thought of it.

"It looks like brown water," groaned Cat.

"That's why you eat it with a straw!" replied Dog.

SLURP! SLURP! SLURP!

"It's hi-ho-diggety-delicious!"

Cat took a sip. "Hmm . . . not bad. Not bad at all."

Cat liked it so much, he had two servings. Dog had eight.

Full and tired after their first big day in space, CatDog was ready for bed. They called Lola on the radio and signed off for the night.

Then CatDog floated over to their special space bed. They had to wear bed belts when they slept so they wouldn't float around all night.

Cat purred happily. "Dog, it doesn't get any better than this. We'll get to Mars. Take some pictures. Collect some rocks, come home, and then, let the good times roll!"

Dog craned his neck to look out a window. "Gee, look at all those stars, Cat! Aren't they the shiniest and brightest things you ever saw?"

"Mmm-hmm," Cat said as he smiled and thought it wouldn't be long before he would be a star, too.

"Nighty-night. Don't let the space bugs bite!" said Dog.

Cat turned off the light, yawned, and closed his eyes.

Tap, tap, tap.

"Stop it, Dog. I'm trying to sleep."

"I'm not doing anything, Cat."

Tap, tap, tap.

"Dog! I mean it! Cut it out!"

"I'm not doing anything!"

"Yes, you are!" said Cat.

"No, I'm not!" said Dog.

Tap, tap, tap.

Cat sat up and turned on the light. "Stop playing games, Dog!"

"I promise, Cat, that wasn't me."

Now Cat knew that when Dog promised something, he meant it. They heard the noise again. Except this time it was closer.

Dog gulped. "It sounds like footsteps. . . ."

"That's impossible," said Cat. "We're the only ones on this ship!"

It was footsteps. It was definitely footsteps. Someone or something was walking around the spaceship.

Cat reached for his radio communicator walkie-talkie.

"Nearburg, we have a problem."

chapter 8

"That's impossible!" said Lola. "No one else can be onboard. I checked every part of that spaceship, every single nook and cranny!"

"Well, something's here, 'cause we can hear it!" said Cat.

"Well, go investigate!" said Lola.

"Okeydokey!" Dog said, unbuckling their bed belt.

"Wait!" said Cat. "Maybe it will go away."

"Stop being such a big baby and go check it out!" said Lola.

"All right," said Cat reluctantly.

Cat and Dog crawled out of their space bed and began to float quietly through the ship.

Dog whispered to Cat, "Gee, I hope it isn't a big, giant, slimy space monster with red scary eyes and long tentacles with big suckers that grab us and put us in its mouth and chew us with razor-sharp teeth for a hundred million years."

"Dog. Don't talk. Just look," said Cat.

CatDog floated through the ship, shining a flashlight into dark corners.

The footsteps were getting louder.

"We're getting closer!" whispered Dog.

"That's what I'm afraid of," replied Cat.

The sound was now coming from right around the corner. CatDog knew that soon they would discover the intruder.

They rounded the corner and came face-to-face with . . .

"A tiny blue space creature!" screamed Dog.

"WINSLOW!" yelled Cat.

"Hiya, CatDog! Where can I get some grub around here? I'm starving!" Winslow said, patting his little blue belly.

"What are you doing here?" demanded Cat.

"Hey, why should you two always have all the fun?" Winslow replied as he floated in the air. "I've never been to Mars, either! I thought I'd tag along."

Cat was furious. Winslow was not his favorite person in the world, and to think of that little pest on their mission and possibly intruding on his fame and fortune was just too much for one Cat to stand!

Dog, on the other hand, was glad to see his friend. "Gee, Cat, it'll be fun to have Winslow with us. He can help."

"Help?" cried Cat. "Help himself to my fame and fortune—that's what he'll do! No way! Forget it! This is a two-man operation. No rats allowed."

Winslow put his hands on his hips. "Hey,

I pay my taxes! I helped pay for this rocket, so I figure I get to tag along for the ride!"

"You're a stowaway!" said Cat angrily. "Dog, throw him in the brig!"

"What's a brig?" asked Dog.

"It's what they call a jail on a ship," replied Cat.

"Do we have one?" asked Dog.

Just then Lola's voice came over the speaker. "This is Nearburg. Have you found out what was making the noise?"

"As a matter-of-fact, we have," replied Cat. "It's a little blue rat named Winslow T. Oddfellow!"

"WINSLOW!" yelled Lola.

"That's exactly what I said!" said Cat. "Listen, Lola, can we make him walk the plank?"

"Hey, this ain't no pirate ship!" objected Winslow.

"Or how about we use him for a highly dangerous experiment that ends in a disaster?" suggested Cat. "Or just shoot him out into space? Or leave him on a planet?"

Just then Dog saw something fly by the window. Cat didn't see it. He was too busy yelling at Winslow.

"Cat!" yelled Dog.

"Quiet, Dog. I'm thinking of cruel and unusual punishments for Winslow!"

"But it's important!" said Dog.

"And having a rat onboard isn't? We need to call the Nearburg Health Department and get an exterminator up here!" said Cat.

"But I really think you should look out the window," said Dog impatiently.

"Dog! You are trying my patience! We will have plenty of time to look out the window and admire the lovely view and contemplate the wonder and majesty of space and the solar system in all its glory. . . ."

Winslow looked out the window. "Hey, whiskers, I'd listen to Dog if I were you!"

"Who asked you, stowaway?" said Cat.

"Cat! Look!" cried Dog.

"I'm sure it's a very pretty sight," said Cat.

"I wouldn't call it pretty!" yelled Dog.

"Well, whatever it is, it can wait. Right now we have an important matter at hand!" said Cat.

"You don't call a meteor shower important?" yelled Dog.

"Meteors . . . ?" asked Cat, suddenly worried. "You don't mean those big, gigantic rocks that fly through outer space and smash into spaceships and destroy all the wonderful people inside?"

"Yes!" said Dog, pointing out the window. "Meteors! And it looks like about a million of them are headed right at us!"

Cat looked out the window. They were headed straight into a meteor shower.

"Way to go, Captain Doofus!" said Winslow.

chapter 9

Down at Mission Control, Rancid was getting upset. "Lola! You said there wouldn't be any meteors this time of year!"

"There aren't supposed to be!" answered Lola. "It's not meteor season yet!"

"Well, Miss Not-So-Smarty-Pants, don't let any of those meteors wreck my ship!"

"Rancid, I can't do anything down here. It's up to CatDog to steer that ship."

"Can they do it?" asked Rancid.

Lola shook her head. "We didn't train CatDog to dodge meteors," she said softly.

Up in the spaceship, Cat was tearing his hair out. "Meteors! We're doomed! We'll be smashed to bits! I'll never get my parade!"

"If there's an escape pod in this bucket, I'd like to volunteer to take it for a test ride!" said Winslow.

Dog was looking at the meteors as they came closer and closer to their ship. Something looked familiar.

"Wait a minute!" yelped Dog. "This is just like my video game, *Mean Bob's Meteor Masher,* that I play on my Dog Boy video game player!"

Cat turned to Dog. "You mean that silly little childish game you're always playing in bed while I'm trying to go to sleep that goes, *Beep!* And, *Boop!* And, *Be-bop-a-lu-la?"*

"Yep!" said Dog excitedly. "And I always beat the game! I bet I can beat these meteorites, too!"

"Like I said, I've always loved that game!" said Cat.

"Give it a shot, hotshot!" chimed in Winslow.

"Zip it, rodent!" said Cat. "I'm calling the shots here." Cat turned to Dog. "Do it, Dog. You're our only hope."

Dog grabbed the controls and started steering in and out of the meteors.

ZIP!

One huge meteor came right at their ship, and Dog expertly dodged it, steering the ship out of the way.

"Here comes another!" yelled Cat.

SWOOSH! Dog dodged the meteor.

"Watch out for that one, Dog!" cried Winslow.

ZOOM!

Dog expertly dodged it, weaving in and out as the meteors zipped past the ship.

"Here come two of them!" cried Cat.

Dog drove right in between them. "Wow!

This is exactly like playing *Mean Bob's Meteor Masher*, except there's no music, no sound effects, it doesn't cost sixty dollars, you don't need batteries, and Mean Bob isn't saying, 'I'm Mean Bob and I'm mad and I make mincemeat out of meteors!'"

Suddenly there were more meteors and they were coming faster and faster right at the ship.

Cat decided it was a good time to hide somewhere.

Rancid's voice came over the loudspeaker. "Be careful with my spaceship! That's a very expensive piece of machinery! They don't grow on trees, you know!"

Lola grabbed the microphone from Rancid. "You be careful, CatDog! We don't want anything bad to happen to you."

Winslow piped up. "Hey! Doesn't anybody care about me?"

"No!" said Cat.

"Just a few more meteors and we're

home safe!" Dog proudly announced.

Dog did a quick-back-double-turn-and-sideways-shift, which was Mean Bob's favorite move, to avoid the last of the meteors. "We made it!" he yelled.

Not one single meteor had hit the spaceship. Dog had successfully dodged them all.

"I wish I knew what my score was!" said Dog.

"I believe it was meteors, zero; Dog, 752!" said Winslow. "Way to go, hero!"

Rancid came on the speaker. "Okay, okay. If you boys are through playing 'dodge the meteors,' you can get back to the mission at hand!"

"Yes, sir, Mr. Rancid, sir!" said Dog.

"Hey, Cat," said Winslow, "you can come out from under that chair now. It's all over!"

Cat came out from under the chair where he had been hiding. "I . . . uh . . . I was just looking for some change I had . . . uh . . . dropped!" he said.

"Yeah, right!" said Winslow.

Cat frowned. He had to face the fact that Winslow was on the ship. He was stuck with the little rat.

"How long till we get to Mars?" asked Winslow.

"About twelve million more miles," said Cat.

"Sheesh Louise! That's gonna take forever!" complained Winslow.

"Actually, since Lola put in a super—" Cat stopped himself. Suddenly he had a brilliant idea of how to rid himself of the blue rodent. "What I meant to say was, you're right, Winslow. It will be a very long trip. A very long, slow, and boring trip."

"Well, that's a stone-cold drag!" said Winslow.

"But we can go—" Dog began.

"Shush, Dog. I'm talking," said Cat.

"Now, Winslow, you could avoid the long, boring trip if we put you in the suspended animation frozen sleep chamber."

"What the heck is that?" asked Winslow.

Cat explained. "You go to sleep, and the machine freezes you. When we get to Mars, we'll defrost you. You'll feel like you had a nice little nap and you'll avoid the whole long, boring trip!"

Winslow nodded his blue head. "Sounds good to me! Where is it?"

Cat pointed, and Winslow hopped into the hibernation sleeping unit. Cat closed the lid, pushed the button, and Winslow settled down for a long snooze in suspended animation.

"Cat, why didn't you tell Winslow that we have an ultra-super-duper-hyper-space-warp-speed that will get us to Mars in about two hours?" asked Dog.

"Because I want that rat out of my hair!" said Cat. "I don't want him running around here bothering us. We'll wake him up when the trip is over!"

Dog looked in at Winslow. "Gee, he sure looks cute in there. Kind of like a little blue frozen Popsicle."

"Yeah. If we run out of food, we can eat him," said Cat.

chapter 10

Two hours later Dog caught sight of their final destination. "Mars, straight ahead!" he cried.

Cat raced to the window. There it was. A red ball floating in space. Waiting for them to land.

"Ten minutes till touchdown," said Lola. "Prepare for landing."

CatDog began to get ready for the landing and their walk on Mars.

Down at Mission Control, Lola suddenly realized something. "We've got a problem,

Rancid. We never decided who was going to be the first one to step onto Mars. Is it Cat or Dog?"

Rancid rubbed his chin. "That won't be a problem. They're best friends!"

CatDog was helping each other get into their space suit and putting on their helmets.

"Cat, there's nobody I'd rather be with on Mars than you, buddy!" Dog said, zipping up his side of the space suit.

"Thanks, pal. They couldn't have picked two better partners," said Cat as he zipped up his side. "Now, when I step out onto the surface of Mars first—"

"You step out first?" said Dog. "I'm going first!"

"No, Dog. I'm going first. We have to go in alphabetical order. C comes before D, therefore I go before you," said Cat.

"Are you sure about that?" questioned Dog.

"Of course I am!" Cat began to sing the alphabet song. "A-B-C-D . . . see? C comes before D!"

"I know my ABCs!" said Dog angrily. "Why do we have to go in alphabetical order?"

"Well . . . uh . . . somebody . . . said . . . uh—" stammered Cat.

"You just made that up! I'm going first!" said Dog.

"You can't!" said Cat.

"Why?" asked Dog.

"Because!" said Cat.

"Because why?" demanded Dog.

"Because I'm older!" said Cat, crossing his arms.

"But I'm braver!" said Dog.

"I'm smarter!" said Cat.

"I'm cuter!" said Dog.

"I'm handsomer!" said Cat.

"CatDog!" said Lola over the loudspeaker.

"I'm faster!" said Dog.

"I'm taller!" said Cat.

"CATDOG!" yelled Lola.

"I'm a dog! I'm man's best friend!"

"I'm a cat! I always land on my feet!"

"CATDOG!" screamed Lola. "Your spaceship is about to crash into Mars!"

CatDog looked out the window in horror as Mars was rushing toward them at a terrifying speed.

"You must lower the landing gear!" yelled Lola.

"Push the button, Dog!" yelled Cat.

"Where's the button?" asked a panicked Dog.

"Right here in front of me!" cried Cat.

Dog reached over and pushed the button. The landing gear slowly began to lower out of the bottom of the spaceship.

"It's too late!" said Cat. "We're gonna crash! I'm never gonna have a parade!"

"Reduce your speed!" called Lola.

Dog pulled a lever back, and they could hear the engines slow down.

"Are we gonna make it, Lola?" asked Dog.

"I don't know!" said Lola.

CatDog grabbed on to each other as the ship hurtled toward Mars.

"Cat, I'm sorry. You can step onto Mars first!" said Dog.

"I don't think it matters anymore, Dog," said Cat.

CatDog closed their eyes.

CRASH!

The Really Rancid Rocket Ship had landed on Mars.

chapter 11

Cat slowly opened his eyes. "Dog?"

Dog slowly opened his eyes. "Cat?"

Cat looked around. "Are we alive?"

Dog pinched himself. "Ow!" He rubbed his arm. "Yeah. We're still alive."

Rancid's voice come over the loudspeaker. "CatDog! Is my spaceship all right?"

"Looks okay to me," said Dog.

"How about you, CatDog? You okay?" asked a concerned Lola.

"We're fine, Lola," said Cat.

Lola ran a quick check on her computers to make sure the ship was okay. Then she gave a very stern lecture to CatDog. "You've got to be careful up there! If you damage the ship, there's no way back! You gotta be able to blast off and come back!"

"Sorry, Lola," said Dog.

"Ditto," said Cat.

"Can we walk on Mars now, Lola? Can we? Can we? Please, please, please?" asked Dog impatiently.

"Yes," replied Lola. "Prepare for the walk. By the way, who's going first?"

Cat and Dog looked at each other.

"Well," said Dog, "Cat can go first."

"If you insist!" said Cat.

The big moment had come. CatDog was about to open the door, go down a ladder, and step onto Mars for the very first time!

They double-checked their space suits to

make sure everything was working. Then Dog pushed a big yellow button, and the door slowly slid open. CatDog was amazed at what they saw.

"Mars! Just like I pictured it!" said Dog.

Mars looked like the biggest desert they had ever seen. There were volcanoes, dry riverbeds, huge valleys, craters, giant rocks, enormous canyons and, off in the distance, dust storms blowing silently over the surface. It looked cold. It looked scary. And it looked very lonely.

And now it was time to step out. They would be the very first human beings—well, the very first CatDog—on Mars.

"Proceed to surface," said Lola over the walkie-talkie inside CatDog's space helmets.

CatDog carefully began to step down the ladder.

"Wait a minute!" said Cat.

"What's the matter?" asked a worried Lola.

"I have to make a phone call," said Cat.

"What? You're about to walk on Mars!" screamed Lola.

"Don't ruffle your feathers, Lola; it'll take five seconds," said Cat as he dialed his cell phone.

Dog was mad too. "Cat! What are you—?"

"Shhh, Dog!" Cat whispered into the phone, "Randolph? It's Cat. We're all set to go."

On the other end, Randolph replied, "Ready when you are, C. D.!"

"Hit it!" said Cat.

chapter 12

Back on Earth, in Nearburg, Randolph was in a TV studio. And the studio was filled with a big audience and a big orchestra.

Randolph was wearing a tuxedo and smiling his pearly white teeth at the camera. "Welcome to *The CatDog on Mars News Special and Good-time Hour*! Featuring me, your very own Randolph Grant, Nearburg's most *exciting* man! We are only *seconds* away from CatDog stepping onto the surface of Mars! I haven't been this excited since the first time I looked into a mirror! I have goose bumps! And I love it! We are now going *live* to MARS!"

"Cat? What's going on?" asked Dog.

Cat pulled a TV camera out of his backpack and turned it on.

"Hello, CatDog! This is Randolph Grant, live in Nearburg! You're on TV!"

Cat blushed. "We're on TV? Oh, my goodness! What a surprise! I had no idea!"

Cat then pulled a top hat out of his pack and put it on top of his space helmet. Dog stood there looking confused.

"Cat! What is going on?" yelled Dog.

Cat shushed him. "Keep your fur on, Dog. Just giving them a little razzle-dazzle!"

Cat delicately stepped onto Mars, and then Dog followed.

"Cat, would you please tell us, in your own words, how it feels to be on Mars?" asked Randolph.

"I'd love to, Randy!" said Cat as he pulled out a little plastic bag that said PIANO on it.

Cat opened the bag, poured some water from a Thermos, and suddenly a grand piano appeared!

Dog could not believe his eyes.

"Dehydrated piano," said Cat nonchalantly, "You just add water."

Cat sat down at the piano and said, "I'd like to dedicate this to the poor, pathetic, little people who can't be here with me."

And then Cat began to play the piano and sing:

"That's one small step for a cat,
And one giant leap for catkind!
When I think of what I did,
It really blows my mind!
Imagine me, a simple cat at birth
And now I am the GREATEST cat on Earth!
I'm Cat! I'm Cat! I'm Caaaaaaaaaaaaattttt!

"That's one small step for a cat,
And one giant leap for catkind!

The first cat on Mars!
I thank my lucky stars!
You have to agree,
It's pretty cool to be ME!
I'm Cat! I'm Cat! I'm Caaaaaaaaaaaaattttt!

"That's one small step for a cat
And one giant leap for catkind!
Up here in space,
I'm a special kind of guy.
I know you'd love to be me,
But don't . . . don't even try!
I'm Cat! I'm Cat! I'm Caaaaaaaaaaaaattttt!"

Cat finished his song and took a big bow.

"I love it!" screamed Randolph as he applauded back in Nearburg. "Well, folks, that's it for CatDog on Mars! So long, CatDog, we'll see you when you get back!"

Cat waved to the camera.

Lola's voice came screeching into Cat's

helmet. "WHAT THE HECK WAS THAT?"

"Just a little quality entertainment," said Cat.

Lola was furious. "Cat! You try anything like that again without telling me and I'll fly up there and I'll grab you and I'll peck you and I'll wring your neck and kick your butt and stomp your—"

"Okay, okay, I get the idea," said Cat calmly as he removed his top hat.

"This is a scientific expedition!" Lola screamed. "Not some Broadway musical! Get back to science! It's time for you to take out the Mars Mobile, get some photographs, collect the rocks—"

Rancid burst in on the speaker, "Don't forget the rocks, boys! Lots and lots of rocks!"

chapter 13

Lola calmed down, and CatDog collected Mars rocks. Actually, Dog did all the work while Cat took pictures. Dog loaded the rocks into the spaceship, filling up the huge storage area till it was jam-packed.

"Can you fit any more rocks in there?" asked Rancid.

"No, sir," said Dog. "Now can we go for a ride in the Mars Mobile, Lola?"

"Yes. Take it out and explore the area," replied Lola.

"Hi-ho-diggety!" exclaimed Dog.

"Wait!" said Cat. "First I want you to take some pictures of me, Dog. I need a great shot that I can autograph and sell to my fans!"

Dog took picture after picture of Cat posing on rocks until Lola yelled at them to stop.

Dog pushed a button on the side of the spaceship. A door slid open, a ramp came down, and out rolled the Mars Mobile. It looked like a giant silver jeep with enormous tires.

Dog hopped into the driver's seat of the Mars Mobile. "Let's see what this baby can do!" he yelled, turning it on.

"Just be careful, Dog," warned Cat. "No crazy driving."

It was too late.

Dog had already put the pedal to the metal, and the Mars Mobile lurched forward and raised up in the air like a bucking bronco—if a bucking bronco had four chrome wheels and fuel injection. The rear tires spun, kicking up a cloud of Mars dust as the Mars Mobile peeled out onto the Mars landscape.

They flew across the sand, zipping up and down canyons, careening through craters, bouncing over rocks.

Finally Cat couldn't take it anymore. "Stop! Dog! Stop!" he commanded.

Dog hit the brakes and turned to Cat. "You wanna go faster?"

"No! I do not want to go faster! I want to go at a normal, safe speed!"

Dog frowned. "But faster is funner!"

Cat pushed Dog out of the driver's seat. "Let a real driver take over." Cat put on his seat belt and adjusted the seat. "Now, observe while an expert, skilled in the art of driving, shows you how it's done!"

Cat grabbed the wheel and pressed down on the accelerator.

"See?" he said, turning toward Dog. "You

drive carefully. Not too fast, not too slow—"

"But shouldn't you be watching the road?" asked a nervous Dog.

"Are you telling me how to drive?" asked Cat.

"No, but I think you should look, because we're about to crash into our spaceship!" yelled Dog.

Cat looked. But it was too late.

They crashed right into the spaceship and heard a horrible *CRUNCH!*

Cat smiled weakly. "Uh, that coulda happened to anybody."

"You wrecked our spaceship!" cried Dog.

"It's just a little dent," said Cat.

"A little dent? You smashed the engines! We have no power!"

Cat nervously switched on his walkie-talkie. "I'm sure it's fine. I'll just call Lola, and she'll tell us what to do."

Cat turned on his communicator. "Nearburg! Come in, Nearburg! Help!"

There was no sound. Cat tried the walkie-talkie again. Nothing. Along with one of the engines the radio antennae had been smashed too. Cat gasped. He just realized that their oxygen tanks would soon be empty if they didn't get the engines going.

For two whole hours, CatDog tried to get the spaceship to start up. They pushed every button they could find. They turned every dial. They flipped every lever. They threw every switch. They flipped every knob. Then they kicked the spaceship. They yelled at it. They yelled at each other. They tried everything, but nothing worked.

CatDog was stuck on Mars—maybe forever.

chapter 14

"We're doomed!" cried Cat as he looked around at the desolate landscape. "So this is how it all ends . . . on this gosh-forsaken planet."

"We can't give up," said Dog.

"Oh, yes, we can! It's easy. You just say, 'I'm giving up!' I'm very good at it. Trust me, it'll save us a lot of time."

"Maybe we can fix the spaceship?" suggested Dog.

"Dog, look at us. Do we look like rocket scientists? We can't even fix a leaky faucet! We certainly can't fix this!"

"But we could try," said Dog, picking up a piece of the ship.

"Forget it, Dog!"

"But there must be something we can do," said Dog.

"There's nothing!" said Cat.

"Cat, we gotta do something! We can't just stand here!" pleaded Dog desperately.

"Well, there *is* one thing you can do, Dog."

"Yeah? What? What is it?" asked Dog anxiously.

"You could cross your eyes, stick one finger in your ear and one finger in your nose, dance a jig on one foot, and sing 'Happy Birthday.'"

Dog immediately crossed his eyes, put one finger in his ear and one finger in his nose, hopped on one foot, started dancing a jig, and sang "Happy Birthday."

"Did that fix the spaceship?" asked Dog excitedly.

"No," said Cat, "but you said you wanted to do something and you might as well do something idiotic because . . . NOTHING WE DO IS GOING TO GET US OFF THIS STINKING PLANET!!!"

"That wasn't very funny, Cat."

"Do you see me laughing?" asked a very mad Cat.

CatDog sat down and fell silent for a long while.

Then Dog quietly spoke. "Gee, I guess we're going to grow old on Mars."

"I don't think so, Dog."

"Why not?"

Cat sighed, "Our oxygen will run out first."

chapter 15

Back in Nearburg, at Mission Control, Rancid watched as Lola frantically tried to contact CatDog. The last thing they had heard was the crash when Cat ran into the spaceship. It sounded like a horrible explosion.

"Come in, CatDog! Please come in! Do you read me? CatDog? CatDog!"

There was no response.

Lola sadly shook her head. "This is a sad day for Nearburg."

"I'll say it is!" said Rancid as he wiped a tear from his eye.

"We've lost something very special," said Lola.

Rancid nodded and blew his nose. "Yes, we have. My beautiful rocket ship!"

"What?" exclaimed Lola. "I'm talking about CatDog! Forget about the spaceship!"

"Forget about it? Do you know how much that thing cost?" said Rancid.

"It doesn't matter! We lost our two dearest friends!" cried Lola.

"And I lost a very expensive spaceship!" said Rancid.

Lola wiped a tear from her eye. "You can always make another spaceship, Rancid, but you can't make another CatDog."

Cat looked up at the stars. "Why do bad things happen to good cats?" he asked.

Dog shrugged his shoulders. "I don't know."

"Why did I ever go on this trip?"

complained Cat. "I should be at home right now, waxing my yarn balls."

"But you wanted to go, Cat," said Dog. "You wanted to be famous and rich and have a parade."

"It ain't worth it," said Cat as he tossed a Mars rock in the sand. "Say, how much more oxygen do we have?"

Dog looked at the meter on their tank. "About thirty minutes' worth."

"Well, Dog," said Cat, "it doesn't get any worse than this."

"Well, Cat, I think it just did!" said Dog, pointing off into the distance.

Something was coming toward CatDog. Something big. Something scary. Something CatDog did not want to see.

"I thought Lola said there weren't any living things on Mars!" said a scared Dog.

"She was wrong!" said a very scared Cat.

The monster or creature or thing or whatever it was came closer. And the closer it got, the scarier it looked.

As it stepped out of the shadows and into the light, CatDog saw the most hideous and terrifying sight they had ever seen—even more hideous and terrifying than the time they saw Rancid Rabbit in a bathing suit!

The thing was a huge creature at least eight feet tall. Its skin was green and purple and blue with pink bumps. It had two long arms—really long arms. The kind of arms that could grab you and do awful things to you.

Its face, if it could even be called a face, had one gigantic blue eye and one gigantic green eye. There were six eyebrows on its forehead. The creature had two ears, one yellow and one red. And finally it had three noses. One big nose, one not-so-big nose, and one small nose. Under each nose was a small mustache.

Cat pushed Dog forward. "Dog, go fight it!"

"Why me?" asked Dog.

"Because!" said Cat.

"Because why?"

"Because you're braver, cuter, faster, and you're man's best friend!"

Dog gave Cat a dirty look. "You go fight it!"

"No!" protested Cat. "I'll stay right behind you and cheer you on."

The Mars monster came closer.

"What do you think it's gonna do to us?" asked Dog.

Cat gulped. "Something very unpleasant!"

As the Mars monster got closer they could hear its feet making loud sucking noises with each step it took.

Slurp! Slurp! Slurp!

The monster opened its mouth. Huge fangs were dripping with yucky white stuff. Cat was sure that it was going to gobble them up in one painful bite. Well, at least it will be a quick end, he thought.

chapter 16

The monster's mouth opened wider and then something very odd happened.

It smiled.

And then it spoke. *"Parlez-vous Français?"*

CatDog didn't move.

The monster spoke again. *"Parlez-vous Français?"*

Dog whispered to Cat, "It's speaking Mars talk!"

"No, Dog, it's French," said an astounded Cat. "It's speaking French!"

"We landed in France instead of Mars?"

asked a befuddled Dog. "Can we see the *Mona Lisa* and the Eiffel Tower?"

"*¿Habla español?*" said the monster.

"That's Spanish," said an even more befuddled Cat.

"We're in Spain?" said Dog. "I wanna run with the bulls and have a tamale!"

"*Sprechen sie deutsch?*" said the monster.

"That's German," said Cat.

"Now we're in Germany? I wanna dance the polka and have some strudel! Yah?"

"Dog, we are not in France or Spain or Germany! We are on Mars!" said an exasperated Cat.

"My goodness! You speak Quadril!" said the monster in a pleasant voice.

Cat replied, "Quadril? No, we speak English. Well, I speak English. Dog's still learning."

The monster raised its eyebrows. "English? Never heard of it. But it sounds exactly like Quadril! They must be the same! What a wild and strange coincidence, and how fortunate for us!"

"Are you going to eat us or kill us?" asked a shaking Dog.

"Or both?" asked a quivering Cat.

"Eat you?" said the Mars monster. "Why on Mars would I want to eat you? No, no, no. I'm a vegetarian. I don't eat meat. Besides, it would be rather unpleasant to eat something that talks to me!"

And then the monster laughed.

And that's when CatDog knew they were safe.

CatDog sighed a huge sigh of relief that could be heard all the way to Pluto, if there was anybody living on Pluto.

The monster smiled and bowed. "Please allow me to introduce myself. My name is Popo Momo. And whom do I have the pleasure of meeting?"

"I'm Cat."

"I'm Dog."

"Pleased to make your acquaintance," said Popo.

"You can call us CatDog," said Dog.

"I shall. Do you come from the planet of CatDogs?" asked Popo.

"No. Is there one?" asked Dog excitedly.

"I don't know. I was just guessing," replied Popo as he scratched his yellow ear.

"We come from a planet called Earth, the third one from the sun," said Cat.

"And everyone looks like you?" asked Popo, scratching his third nose.

"No, no, no. There's only one CatDog," said Cat proudly.

Pop leaned forward and looked at CatDog closer. "You know, you remind me of my cousins, Zaneeta and Ulaylee."

And when Popo said that, he began to sniffle and whimper and then he began to cry. Tears poured from his eyes. He blew his noses, one at a time. His little nose made a high noise, his big nose made a low noise, and the middle-sized nose made a noise somewhere in between.

"I'm sorry," Popo said, sniffling. "It is just so very sad."

"Did something happen to your cousins?" asked Dog.

"Yes! I mean, no! Something happened to me. It's a sad story. I used to have lots of cousins and uncles and aunts and grandparents and friends. And now they're all gone. Gone with the wind!"

"The wind blew them away?" asked Dog.

"Well, in a manner of speaking, yes. I'll explain," said Popo as he arranged his three noses so they hung just right. "Mars used to be a wonderful place to live. Lovely climate. Sunshine. Warm rain. We'd go sailing in the canals. We'd play games like schnibbie, and Pin the Smatta On The Twarkluff, read books, go to all-night Ping-Pong parties, and eat squalarks and race bowrafs and go surfing—"

"You surf!" exclaimed Dog.

Popo nodded. "Oh yes. It's the national pastime of Mars."

"So why did everybody leave?" asked Cat.

Popo smiled a sad little smile. "About three hundred moonrises ago, the great dust storm came. Great clouds of red dust blowing so hard, you couldn't see your three noses in front of your face. So Jim-Jam, the great pooh-bah, leader of Mars, and a very good surfer, incidentally, decided we would all pack up and move to Mercury. Land is cheap, it's nice and hot, and the surfing is incredible."

"Why didn't you go?" asked Dog.

"Didn't you want to?" asked Cat.

"Want to? Of course I wanted to!" said Popo. "Everyone wanted to and everyone was going. We had all built a gigantic spaceship so big, it could hold all three million of us for the trip to Mercury."

"And did it go to Mercury?" asked Dog.

"Yes! Except I wasn't on it," said Popo, who started to sniffle again.

"Why not?" asked Dog.

Cat whispered to Dog, "Stop interrupting!"

Popo continued. "I'll tell you. The night we were to leave I stayed up late packing. I was so nervous and excited and anxious that I forgot to set my alarm clock."

"But didn't anyone notice you were missing?" asked Cat.

"No," replied Popo. "There were three million of us. I guess all my friends and family thought I was onboard. I think by the time they figured out I wasn't there, it was too late. You see, it was a one-way trip. We had just enough fuel to get to Mercury. What woke me up was the sound of the rocket blasting off. I looked at my clock, and you can imagine how I felt! I grabbed my suitcase and ran as fast as I could, but when I got there the ship was already blasting off. I just stood there and watched all my friends and family sail away into space."

Popo began to cry again.

Dog was crying too. "That's the saddest story I've ever heard!"

"So you're the very last man on Mars," said Cat.

"Yes, I haven't seen anyone since you came. . . . Hey, wait! What am I thinking? How did you get here?" asked Popo anxiously.

"We came in a spaceship," said Cat.

"A spaceship?" said Popo. "A spaceship! Splendid! You could give me a ride to Mercury! Will you? Please? Oh, hooray! You have a ship!"

"We have a broken spaceship," said Cat quietly.

Popo's face clouded over. "Broken?"

Cat looked down at the Mars dust. "Uh . . . we had a little accident."

"Cat had a little accident. He broke our spaceship!" said Dog.

Cat gave Dog a dirty look. "You see, Popo, there was an unavoidable accident. We're not quite sure exactly what happened."

"Yes, we are!" said Dog. "You crashed the Mars Mobile into the engine!"

Cat ignored Dog. "We don't know exactly how it happened."

"Yes, we do! You weren't looking where you were going!" said Dog.

"All right, Dog! Enough already! The point is, the spaceship doesn't work anymore. So we're stuck here on Mars, too."

"How badly is it broken?" asked Popo.

"Really bad! Cat smashed it up!" said Dog.

"Dog!"

"He asked me, Cat!"

Cat turned to Popo. "Popo? May I call you Popo, or do you prefer Mr. Momo?"

"Please, call me Popo."

Just then a buzzer went off. CatDog's supply of oxygen had run out. They had forgotten all about that since meeting Popo.

"Oh, no! We're out of oxygen!" cried Cat.

"Out of oxygen?" asked Popo.

"I can't breathe!" yelled Dog.

"Yes, you can," said Popo. "Just take off those helmets and you'll breathe fine."

CatDog slowly removed their helmets and breathed in the Mars air. They could breathe! The air was thin and tasted like cinnamon, but there was oxygen!

That was one problem out of the way.

"Well, Popo," said Cat, "since we're gonna be around here for a while, do you know any card games? Old Maid? Go Fish?"

"No, I don't know those games," replied Popo, who seemed to be getting excited, "but I do know how to fix a spaceship!"

"How to Fix a Spaceship?" asked Cat curiously. "I don't know how to play that game, but I suppose since we'll be here a long time you can teach us. How do you play?"

"No, no, no! It's not a card game!" said Popo. "At the University of Mars I studied music, but I took a night class in spaceship maintenance for the easy grade!"

CatDog could not believe their ears. Their mouths hung open.

"You can fix our spaceship?" asked Cat.

"I could try!" said Popo.

"Hi-ho-fix-ety!" yelped Dog.

"Do you think you can fix the radio, too?" asked Cat.

"Maybe," said Popo. "I took a night class in space radio repair once because there was this really cute girl in the class. She had the biggest noses you'd ever seen!"

chapter 17

For three hours Popo worked on the spaceship. As he worked, Dog handed him tools and Cat sat next to them making plans.

Cat could not believe his good fortune. Here was a real, live, honest-to-goodness, no foolin' man from Mars! Cat could make history with this creature. Better than that, he could make millions!

Cat plotted it out in his mind. First, Popo would have to fix the ship. Then Cat would have to persuade Popo to go back with them to Earth. Cat decided he would have to get

Popo back secretly, because he knew that if Lola saw Popo she'd put him in a laboratory and study him. But more importantly, if Rancid Rabbit found out they had a man from Mars, he'd grab him and do *exactly* what Cat wanted to do.

Just then Popo began to sing as he worked. He had a beautiful voice. But Cat noticed he wasn't opening his mouth!

"Popo, are you a ventriloquist?" asked Cat.

"No. I'm a, or at least I used to be, a singer in the Mars Opera Company," said Popo proudly.

"A singer? Opera?" said an impressed Cat.

"Yes. I was first tenor, second bass, and third baritone," said Popo proudly.

"But how could you be all those things at the same time?" said Cat.

"Like this," Popo said, and then he proceeded to sing with his noses!

One nose sang low and deep, like a bass. One nose sang higher notes, like a tenor. And one nose sang in the middle, like a baritone.

Cat shook his head in disbelief. Popo was getting to be more valuable by the minute! A man from Mars who could sing! Three parts at once! Through his noses! Cat had found the gold mine of all gold mines. He could get very rich in his sleep.

But Cat knew that Popo wouldn't be much good stuck here on Mars. Popo had to fix that spaceship.

Popo tightened one last screw. "Well, that's all I know how to do. I hope it works, but I can't guarantee anything. We might as well try it, Dog."

Dog turned the key.

Nothing.

Dog tried it again.

Nothing.

Cat tried it.

Nothing.

Popo tried.

"I'm sorry," said Popo.

"That's okay. You tried," said Dog.

"Turr-rific!" said Cat sarcastically. "Say, Popo, what grade did you get in your How to Fix a Spaceship class? An F?"

"No, I got an A minus," said Popo. "On the last test I missed one question. I forgot that if all else fails, you kick the engine as hard as you can. . . ."

He lifted his leg and kicked the spaceship as hard as he could, stubbing his toe very badly. "Ow! Yikes! Darn it! Dagnabit!" he yelled.

But neither Cat nor Dog could hear a word he said—because the spaceship engines had started up!

chapter 18

"You fixed it, Popo!" cried Dog. "Now we can take you to Mercury so you can be with all your friends and family!"

"Really?" said Popo.

"I promise!" said Dog.

Cat had to think quickly. This was not going according to his plan. He had to get Popo to Nearburg.

"Uh . . . wait a minute," said Cat. "We don't have enough fuel to go all the way to Mercury and then all the way back to Nearburg. Sorry, Popo."

Popo rubbed his noses for a moment. "But if we get rid of all those rocks in your ship, it won't weigh so much and we'll get more miles to the gallon and we can easily make it!"

"Next stop, Mercury!" shouted Dog.

Dog and Popo immediately started throwing all the Mars rocks off the ship. Cat had to think of a new plan—quickly!

As Dog threw the last rock out of the ship, he said, "Now you can fix the radio, Popo, and we can tell Lola and Rancid about you!"

Cat panicked. He had to think fast. "Wait! Before we do that, Dog, you need to check on Winslow. Make sure he doesn't have frostbite. I need to talk to Popo about something."

"Sure, Cat!" said Dog as he stretched over to check on Winslow.

Cat quickly began whispering to Popo. "Just in case you ever change your mind and decide to go with us to Nearburg and continue your singing career, I'd like to be your manager. Watch out for you, protect you, make sure no one takes advantage of you."

"How sweet of you, Cat," said Popo. "But I want to go to Mercury."

"I know. But could you sign this just in case you do change your mind someday? Please? Pretty please? It would make me so happy," said Cat. He held up a contract. Cat had to get Popo to sign it before Rancid and Lola found out about him!

"Well, I won't change my mind," said Popo, "but, sure, for you, Cat, I'll sign!"

"Thank you!" said Cat. "And let's keep this just between you and me. We'll surprise Dog later. He loves surprises!"

Popo signed. Cat noticed he had very good penmanship—another plus! Cat quickly hid the contract when Dog returned.

"Winslow looks okay to me," said Dog. "A little bluer than usual."

"Excellent!" said Cat.

"Shall I fix the radio now?" asked Popo.

chapter 19

At Mission Control, Lola and Rancid had fallen asleep on the radio console. Rancid was dreaming about his sixth-grade teacher, Miss Pippin. Lola was dreaming about CatDog floating in space, when suddenly she heard, "Nearburg! Come in, Nearburg!"

Lola opened her eyes and sat up. It was Dog! CatDog was alive! "CatDog! You're alive! Thank goodness!" she said.

"And guess what? We found something really cool on Mars!" announced Dog.

Rancid's eyes lit up. "What? What? What? Gold? Diamonds? Cute little space bunnies?"

"No, we found—" Dog began.

"How are my rocks?" interrupted Rancid.

"Well, we sorta had to throw them off the ship," said Dog.

"WHAT?" screamed Rancid. "You get those rocks back on that ship right now! I'm selling those rocks for one hundred thousand dollars apiece on the One Bunny Hop-Stop Shopping Network!"

"So that's why you wanted so many darn rocks!" said Lola. "You don't care about science!"

"Hey, a rabbit's gotta make a living!" said Rancid. "Bring me my rocks, CatDog!"

"But if we do that we won't be able to take Popo to Mercury," said Dog.

"Who the heck is Popo?" asked Rancid.

"What the heck is a Popo?" asked Lola.

"This!" said Dog as he aimed the camera

at Popo, who waved and smiled. "Meet Popo Momo!"

"Hello! Pleased as punch to make your acquaintance!" said Popo cheerfully.

Lola and Rancid stood staring at the screen. They couldn't believe what they saw.

A real, live alien.

"I have to study him!" said Lola.

"I have to exploit him!" said Rancid.

"I'm going to win the Scientist of the Century prize!" said Lola.

"I'm going to make a billion dollars!" said Rancid.

Dog leaned into the camera. "We're taking Popo to Mercury to join his friends and then we'll come home. See ya!"

"Wait!" yelled Rancid. "You are to return to Nearburg immediately with that alien!"

"Yes, CatDog! Bring him back!" cried Lola.

Cat pushed his way in front of the

camera. "Just so you two know, I'm Popo's manager. I have an exclusive contract." Cat waved the contract in front of the camera. "If you want to get in on the 'Popo business,' you have to talk to me!"

"WAIT A MINUTE!" screamed Dog at the top of his lungs. "I promised Popo I'd take him to Mercury."

"We're not running a space taxi service!" barked Rancid. "I'm in charge here! Bring him back to Nearburg!"

"We are working for Rancid, Dog," said Cat. "We have to do what he says."

"But I made a promise!" said Dog.

"Look, Mr. Do-Gooder," said Rancid coldly, "I paid for this mission and I say bring Peepee back to Nearburg!"

"His name is Popo!" said Dog.

Popo looked like he was going to start crying again.

Cat tried to look sad for Dog, but he was happy. Now they could return to Earth, and

Cat would be an even bigger hero for returning with a real Mars man, and he was Popo's manager!

Dog tried to explain what had happened to Popo, how everyone had left him there all alone on Mars. How all his family and friends were gone. Lola started to feel sorry for Popo, but Rancid didn't care.

"Bring me Pupu!" barked Rancid.

"It's Popo!" said Dog.

"Whatever! Bring him to me! That's an order!" yelled Rancid.

Cat shrugged. "Orders are orders, Dog. I guess we have to take him back to Nearburg."

"Like heck we do!" said Dog defiantly. "We're going to Mercury, and no one's gonna stop us!"

"Listen up, Dog, and listen good! You are about to get into some serious stinky doo-doo!" said Rancid.

Dog's eyes narrowed, and he spoke

directly into the camera to Rancid and Lola. "Listen up, Rancid, and listen good, 'cause I'm only gonna say this one more time! We are proceeding to Mercury to return Popo to his people! Then we are returning to Nearburg! Over and out!"

chapter 20

The radio at Mission Control went dead.

Rancid yelled at Lola, "Do something! Get them back here! Push some button!"

Lola shook her head. "I can't do anything. They're in control of the ship. They can take it anywhere they want to go. And if you want my opinion—"

"I don't!" said Rancid.

Lola continued. "Well, I'm gonna give it to you! I think they're doing the right thing!"

"Well, I'm gonna send someone up to get

that darn CatDog and bring back that Mars man!" said Rancid.

"How? In what?" asked Lola.

"Don't you have any other spaceships lying around at the office?" wondered Rancid.

"No," said Lola. "The only thing I have is the very first spaceship I built. It wasn't tested. It's too dangerous. It's unsafe at any speed."

"Use it!" said Rancid.

"We can't go up in that!" said Lola.

"Who said anything about us? We'll send someone else up."

"Who?" asked Lola.

"I know the perfect group!" said Rancid.

Back in the spaceship, a grateful Popo said, "CatDog, I can't tell you how much I appreciate this."

"A promise is a promise!" said Dog. "Cat, set your coordinates for Mercury!"

Cat sighed as he set the controls for Mercury. He knew he couldn't change Dog's mind. Once Dog made up his mind like this, there was no stopping him. They would have to take Popo home to all his family and friends.

Cat was just about to tear up the contract, when all of a sudden he got a great idea! When they got to Mercury he might be able to convince one of the other Mars people to go with him to Earth. After all, there were three million of them. At least one of them would want to go to Nearburg!

Cat quickly erased Popo's name off the contract to save it for later and thought, You are one smart cat, Cat!

"I'm setting the controls to ultra-super-duper-hyper-space-warp-speed," announced Dog. "Here we go!"

Thirty-seven seconds later, Mercury came into sight.

"There it is!" cried Dog, slowing the spaceship down.

"My new home, sweet home!" said Popo. "Oh, thank you, CatDog! Thank you, thank you, thank—"

"Unidentified spacecraft on starboard side!" shouted Cat.

Dog and Popo raced to the window to see an odd-looking spaceship hurtling toward them.

"Who's that?" asked Popo.

"I don't know, but I'm gonna find out," said Dog as he got on the interspace radio. "Hey, there! You in the strange-looking spaceship. Please identify yourself!"

The radio crackled. "We are the . . . uh . . . Greaserians."

Cat scratched his head, "Greaserians? That sounds familiar."

"Where are you from, Greaserians?" asked Dog.

After a very long pause, the voice on the radio spoke again. "Uh . . . we are from Grease!"

"You mean the country Greece, where the Olympics came from?" asked Cat.

"No! The planet Grease. G-r-e-a-s-e," said the voice.

"Grease?" wondered Cat. "I've never heard of that planet. Have you, Popo?"

Popo shook his head.

"Uh . . . it's a new planet," said the voice. "We just opened it."

A different, higher-pitched voice came over the radio. "We request permission to board your ship!"

"Are you friendly aliens?" asked Dog.

"Yeah! Sure we are!" replied the voice. "And we wish to bring you flowers, gifts, and stuff like that."

Cat turned to Popo. "What do you think?"

Popo rubbed his second nose. "Well, I love flowers and gifts, so I say, why not!"

Cat thought to himself, Maybe I could take these aliens back to Earth.

"Something smells fishy," said Dog.

"That's me," apologized Popo.

"Then it's settled!" said Cat. "Permission to board is granted!"

The strange ship slowly docked next to CatDog's ship. A door on the side opened, and a special airtight tunnel poked out and connected to CatDog's ship. This way, the aliens could walk from one spaceship to the other. CatDog and Popo stood at the portal as three figures came out of the darkness.

Cat chuckled to himself as he tried to make out the silhouettes approaching them. Gee, he thought, if we weren't millions of miles from Earth, I would say that was Cliff, Shriek, and Lube!

The aliens came forward into the light.

"Cat!" exclaimed Dog. "Those aliens look just like Cliff, Shriek, and Lube. Wow! What are the odds of that happening?"

"Dog! That is Cliff, Shriek, and Lube!" cried Cat.

chapter 21

"You know these creatures?" asked Popo.

"Yes!" said Cat.

"Ah," said Popo, "so you've been to the planet Grease?"

"There is no planet Grease! They're from our hometown, Nearburg," said Cat.

"How sweet!" said Popo. "They've come to pay a visit!"

Cliff grinned. "Yeah. We came for a little visit. We missed you guys."

Shriek sniggered. "Yeah, we got lonesome."

Lube nodded. "Duh . . . and Rancid said we should come up here and steal dat Mars guy from you and take him back to Nearburg and we will get a big reward."

Cliff turned to Lube and glared. "Lube! Why did you have to make sense for the first time in your whole life!"

Dog leaped in front of Popo. "You're not taking Popo!"

"And who's gonna stop us?" demanded Cliff. "You and your little pussycat?"

"Yeah! Me and my little pussycat!" said Dog, baring his teeth.

"Can we please not refer to me as a 'little pussycat'!" said Cat.

The Greasers started moving toward them.

Cat tugged on one of Popo's arms. "Uh, Popo, if you have any superpowers like the ability to zap someone, or melt them, or disintegrate them, this would be a really good time to use them!"

Popo whispered to Cat, "Sorry. I could beat them at Ping-Pong, but that's about it."

"Well, then," said Cat, "there's only one thing to do . . . RUN!"

CatDog ran away as the Greasers followed in hot pursuit. But it was a very short chase because the spaceship wasn't that big. When it was over and the dust settled, the Greasers had Popo trapped in a bag and CatDog tied up in a knot.

"See ya later, CatDog!" Shriek said, laughing.

"And just so you don't try to follow us," said Cliff, "I think I'll remove this little steering thingamabob right here so you can't! Ha! Ha! Ha!"

And with that, Cliff pulled a very important-looking piece out of the steering wheel.

"Sorry it has to end this way, Doggie," Shriek whispered to Dog. "But every time I look up at the stars, I'll think of you."

"Help!" yelled Popo from inside the bag.

"We'll save you, Popo!" cried Dog.

"Dat's gonna be pretty hard when you're floating out in space till the end of time!" said Cliff.

The Greasers carried Popo onto their ship and sped away. CatDog could only watch helplessly through a window as the Greaser ship disappeared on its way back to Earth.

Cliff was on the radio talking to Rancid. "This is Cliff to Rancid! I got your alien right here."

"Nice work, fellas!" said Rancid.

Shriek barked into the microphone, "I ain't no fella, fella!"

"Sorry, Shriek," said Rancid. "What about CatDog?"

Cliff laughed. "I don't think you have to worry about CatDog anymore."

chapter 22

Back in their spaceship CatDog had untied themselves and were trying to fix their broken steering wheel.

"It *might* work," said Cat, "if we could just jam something the exact same size in this space. But it would have to fit perfectly!"

CatDog frantically looked around the spaceship, but nothing would fit. Everything was either too big or too small.

Suddenly Dog spotted something. "Hey, Cat, can it be something small and short and blue?"

"Small, short, and blue? What are you talking about?"

"Winslow!" said Dog.

Cat grinned. In an instant, CatDog floated over to the frozen chamber that Winslow was in and cracked it open.

"Dreamtime's over, rat boy!" said Cat as he grabbed Winslow.

Woken by Cat's quick motion, Winslow opened his eyes and was alarmed to see that he was headed toward a hole in the steering wheel of the ship.

"Mmmph . . . mmmph," he protested. Winslow couldn't say a word, as his mouth was frozen!

Cat jammed him into the little spot in the steering mechanism. It was a perfect fit into the tiny space. Now their steering wheel worked!

"Well, Winslow, you're finally good for something!" said Cat as he closed the little door on Winslow.

Dog grabbed the controls, and off they sped after the Greasers.

Meanwhile, in the Greaser spaceship, Cliff was staring at Popo, "So you're a man from Mars?"

"Yes, I am. And I think you are behaving quite rudely!" said Popo. "What do you intend to do with me?"

"We're taking you back to Rancid Rabbit," said Shriek.

"And what will he do with me?" asked Popo.

"Make a zillion dollars!" said Shriek.

"And what about you? What will you get?" asked Popo.

"A nice fat reward!" Cliff said, chuckling.

chapter 23

"We're about five minutes away from the Greasers' ship," said Dog.

"Exactly how do you expect to save Popo?" asked Cat.

"Easy!" said Dog excitedly. "This is just like the scene in my second favorite movie of all time, *Mean Bob Versus Evil Eric—The Early Years,* when he saves Princess Kitaen."

"I think I fell asleep during that one," said Cat.

"Well," began Dog, "one of us has to stay inside and steer the ship and one of us has gotta go out into space, get on to the Greaser ship, get inside, fight off the Greasers, get Popo, go back out into space, and come back here."

"I volunteer to stay inside and steer," said Cat.

"Okay, then, I'll be the other guy," said Dog, getting into the space suit.

"But, Dog, how do we get close enough? The Greasers will see our ship!" said Cat.

"Ooops. I forgot," said Dog sadly. "Mean Bob had a button that made his spaceship invisible."

"Like this?" Cat said, pointing at a tiny little button on the control panel, way off in the back, that said, "INVISIBLE SHIELD FOR MAKING SPACESHIP INVISIBLE FOR TWO MINUTES."

"Gee, I wonder why Lola never told us about that button, Cat?"

"Who cares? Use it!" cried Cat.

Dog got ready to push the button. "Okay!

We've got two minutes. Ready? Go!"

Dog pushed the button, and their ship became invisible. Cat steered right up next to the Greasers, and they couldn't see them!

Cat looked over at the Greasers' ship, "Can we really stretch that far, Dog?"

"We have to, Cat!" said Dog as he snapped his helmet shut and went out the air lock into space.

The Greasers had let Popo out of the bag. He was tied up in a corner, and each Greaser took a turn watching him.

Now, Popo had many amazing skills. He could hold his breath for a year. He could count to a million in ten seconds. He could do a perfect cartwheel. And he could see things when they were invisible. So he saw CatDog's spaceship coming closer to rescue him. He knew he had to distract the Greasers so he could escape.

"So this Rancid fellow is giving you all a big reward for bringing me back?" asked Popo innocently.

"Dat's right, slimy!" said Cliff.

"And you'll split it three ways?" asked Popo.

"Dat's the Greaser code!" said Cliff.

Lube nodded. "Duh . . . right! Three ways! One for Cliff, one for Shriek, and one for . . . for . . . for . . . ?"

Dog was stretched across space between the two spaceships. Cat was still inside the ship, holding on to the steering wheel and trying to steer slow and steady.

It was Shriek's turn to watch Popo. Cliff was steering the spaceship, and Lube was trying to remember his name.

Popo smiled at Shriek. "You look like

you're the smartest Greaser."

"'Course I am!" said Shriek.

"You certainly were clever kidnapping me like that. I bet you planned the whole thing."

Shriek smiled proudly. "As a matter of fact, I did!"

"Too bad you have to share that reward money with Cliff and Lube," said Popo, shaking his head.

"Whaddaya mean?"

"You did all the real work. They just came along for the ride. You should get all the reward."

Shriek started to think.

"Hey, Shriek!" shouted Cliff. "It's your turn to drive. I'll watch the three-nose guy now."

Dog carefully and quietly opened the Greasers' air lock hatch so he could get inside their ship. It squeaked as he turned it. He hoped the Greasers didn't hear it. He had to hurry. He only had one minute left!

Shriek took her turn driving.

Popo whispered to Cliff, who was sitting beside him, "You're the leader of the Greasers, right?"

"Dat's very completely true!" said Cliff proudly.

"So why are you sharing the reward? If it wasn't for your brute strength, I wouldn't even be here. You really deserve it all."

"Yeah . . . I do," said Cliff as he turned to Shriek. "Hey, Shriek. I wanna talk to you."

As Shriek and Cliff started to argue, Popo called over to Lube. "Lube, you're the heart and soul of the Greasers. You're doing all the work. Why should you share anything with Cliff and Shriek? If I were you, I'd tell them that you want all the reward."

Lube looked at Popo for a long time, and then spoke. "What reward?"

Dog had made it inside the Greasers' ship. He could hear Cliff and Shriek arguing as he snuck up toward Popo. It was getting harder and harder to stretch the farther he went. He hoped that Cat could hold on.

"I'm the leader!" yelled Cliff. "I'm taking all the reward!"

"It was my plan! I want it all!" Shriek yelled back.

Cliff and Shriek started fighting.

Popo nudged Lube. "You should get in there and fight, Lube!"

"Duh . . . why?" asked Lube.

"Because if you don't, I won't be able to escape," said Popo.

"Okay . . . I go fight. Good-bye. Have a nice escape," said Lube as he dove into the fight.

All three Greasers were now in a ferocious battle, fighting among themselves as Dog snuck up to Popo. Dog quickly untied him, and they quietly began to sneak off the ship. They were almost to the hatch when one of Popo's noses accidentally banged into a cup and knocked it over.

BANG!

Dog and Popo hid in the shadows.

The only Greaser who heard it was Lube, who waved at Dog and Popo and then went back to fighting.

Meanwhile, in the other spaceship, Cat was barely holding on to the steering wheel. He was afraid that Dog was going to stretch too far and something really horrible would happen. Cat knew he couldn't hold on much longer. And in twenty seconds their spaceship would become visible again!

Cat looked out the window and suddenly

saw Dog and Popo floating out of the Greasers' ship. Cat began pulling them back in as fast as he could.

As soon as they closed their hatch and were safe, Dog yelled, "Go, Cat, go!"

And right then their ship became visible again!

The Greasers were too busy fighting to notice, except for Lube. He saw CatDog's spaceship appear, seemingly out of nowhere.

"Duh . . . that's funny," he said. He started to tell Cliff and Shriek about it, but hearing them yelling and screaming about reward money made him forget what he was going to say.

The Greasers continued to fight each other for three hours and twenty-seven minutes before they realized that Popo had left.

"Dat guy with the three noses is gone!" barked Cliff.

"Now we ain't gonna get a reward!" complained Shriek.

"Duh . . . is that bad?" asked Lube.

chapter 24

"Mercury, dead ahead!" announced Cat.

Popo rushed to the window to see a bright yellow ball hanging in space.

"There it is!" cried Popo. "Mercury! My new home, sweet home!"

They could see Mars people surfing.

"Wow! It looks hot down there," said Dog.

"It's about four hundred twenty-six degrees," said Popo.

"Break out the sunblock," said Cat.

CatDog executed a perfect landing onto Mercury. Thousands of Mars people rushed up to see the strange ship land.

When Popo came out the door, he saw all his friends and family. They ran up to greet him. They cried and laughed and hugged, and a few even did cartwheels.

They didn't all look like Popo. Some were short and tall, and some were fat and small. Some were quite handsome in an alien kind of way. Some only had one nose. Some had four noses. One had seventeen.

Popo held up his long arms to quiet down the crowd. "I want you to meet my new friend and the hero who saved my life and brought me back to you . . . CatDog!"

CatDog poked their heads out the door, and everyone cheered.

That night they had a huge celebration. They made speeches, they danced, Popo sang a three-part solo, Cat played his dehydrated piano, and Dog taught everyone the Macarena.

At the party, Cat remembered his contract. He had to get a Martian back to Earth! He asked 427 of the Mars people to go back with him to Nearburg for the chance to be famous and rich and have Cat as their manager.

Much to his dismay, all 427 Mars people politely turned him down. They all loved being on Mercury and wanted to stay. Cat was about to throw a fit, but then realized that he couldn't really take anybody away from a place they loved. He himself wouldn't want to leave Nearburg unless he had a very good reason.

So Cat was disappointed, but the next morning he quickly cheered up. To his great delight and surprise, they had a parade—for CatDog! CatDog got to ride on a float, and all the Mars people waved and clapped their hands and cheered.

"It doesn't get any better than this, Dog!" said Cat.

All too soon it was time to say good-bye. Popo walked with CatDog back to their spaceship.

"Well, Popo, all good things must come to an end," said Cat.

"I shall never forget you," said a teary-eyed Popo. "I wish you didn't have to leave. Are you sure you wouldn't like to stay here?"

"Thanks. But our home is Nearburg," said Cat.

"All our friends are there," said Dog.

"Good-bye, Popo," said Cat.

"Good-bye, CatDog, and thank you," said Popo.

CatDog started walking slowly into their spaceship.

"Thanks for helping me take Popo back to his friends and family," said Dog.

Cat sighed. "Well, I guess some things are more important than fame and fortune."

Suddenly a voice behind them sounded out. "Wait!"

It was Popo. "Wait! My cousins just got here! Zaneeta and Ulaylee! I want you to meet them before you go."

CatDog turned around and saw something they had never seen except when they looked in their mirror:

A two-headed creature.

One body.

Four feet and two heads.

Two beautiful heads.

"Hello, CatDog," cooed Zaneeta.

"We wanted to thank you for returning our dear Popo," said Ulaylee in a sweet, soft voice. "You are *so* brave."

"And *so* handsome," added Zaneeta. "We're sorry you have to go right now. We would have loved to get to know you better."

Cat looked at Dog.

Dog looked at Cat.

And they knew just what they had to do.

Back in Nearburg, Lola was at Mission Control when the radio crackled and she heard Cat's voice.

"CatDog to Nearburg! Come in, Nearburg, this is CatDog on Mercury!"

"CatDog, this is Nearburg!" said Lola. "Are you all right?"

"We're fine and dandy! Couldn't be better! We have returned Popo to his friends and family," said Dog.

"Good. I'm glad. You did the right thing," said Lola. "We are looking forward to your return!"

"Uh . . . yeah, well, about our return. We'll actually be staying on Mercury for a while," said Cat.

"Staying? Why? Is there something wrong?" asked Lola.

"Oh, no, no," said Cat. "It's just that we have some experiments to do."

"What kind of experiments?" Lola asked.

"Interspace relationships," said Cat.

And before Lola could say anything more, Dog called out, "This is CatDog signing off!"

Cat turned off the radio and smiled at Dog. Then he turned to Zaneeta and Ulaylee. "Ladies, I think this is the beginning of a beautiful friendship!"

And then Cat and Dog and Zaneeta and Ulaylee strolled off into the Mercury sunset.

epiLogue

And what happened to the Greasers? Well, when they realized they didn't have Popo onboard anymore, they panicked. They knew Rancid would be very angry if they didn't return with a man from Mars. So they decided to dress Lube up as a Mars man. They gave him three ears, two extra noses, shaved off all his hair, and painted him green. They fooled Rancid—for about one second.

And Rancid? After realizing that he didn't have a Martian man to exploit, he turned his attention to trying to sell phony Martian rocks—but was quickly arrested for selling the rocks without a license.

And Lola? She took the spaceship the Greasers had used, went to Mercury herself, and filmed a documentary about the surfing Mars people. She won the Nearburg Award for Best Documentary Film Made by a Bird About Surfing Mars People on Mercury.

And Winslow? He finally pulled himself out of the spaceship's steering mechanism and, through a very strange turn of events, became king of Mercury. But that's another story.

About the Author

Steven Banks is a writer and actor who plays a number of musical instruments and writes scripts and songs for the CatDog television series. He is the author of the CatDog chapter books *CatDog's Vacation* and *CatDog Undercover.* Steven has also had his own television series aired on PBS called *The Steven Banks Show,* and a special on Showtime called *Home Entertainment Center.*

When he was a kid, Steven and his family watched every single blastoff of the Mercury Space program and once even made what he says was "a very cool space capsule!" He lives in Glendale, California.